Harriet the Hedgehog

Written by Victoria Brock

For Harrison, Megan, Gracie, Sophie,
Martha and Jacob with love.

Illustrated by Kim Whittingham

Harriet the Hedgehog
is very, very shy.
You see, she has no spikes
and she's unsure why...

Her mother has always said,
"You were born this way,
and don't get upset about
what other hogs say."

But Harriet is embarrassed about
the way that she looks.
So instead of going outside she
just sits and reads books.

She watches her sisters
all go out to play,
and secretly hopes,
that it will be her one day.

Then one morning when the birds
were singing outside,
her mum entered her room and said,
"the day has arrived."

"For what?" Harriet asked
excited and afraid.
"It's your first day at school,
so you need to be brave."

So Harriet got herself dressed
and she cleaned her teeth too,
and then she sat, and she wondered
what the other hogs would do.

Would they point, would they laugh,
would they whisper, would they stare?
She wouldn't find out until
she got herself there.

But when Harriet arrived
and walked into the school hall,
not one of the hogs laughed at her at all.
Some of them waved, or said "hello",
one even said, "I wish my spikes would go."

So from that day on
Harriet loved her soft skin,
and she realised that being different,
didn't mean she wouldn't fit in.

About the Author

Victoria grew up in Colchester but she now lives in Bury St Edmunds with her four year old son Jacob. Victoria started writing from a young age and when her son was born she enrolled on a creative writing course and started writing children's books.

Victoria was inspired to write Harriet the Hedgehog when her nieces Megan and Gracie who are identical twins were diagnosed with leukaemia in September 2009 within a week of each other when they were four years old. Their strength and determination has been inspirational and Victoria is pleased to say they are now happy healthy nine year olds.

£1.00 of every copy of Harriet the Hedgehog sold goes to Starlight Children's Foundation who make wishes come true for seriously ill children.

Other books by Victoria are:

Harrison the Hedgehog

Olly the Octopus

Simon the Snake

Reuben the Reindeer

Please see Victoria's website www.victoriabrockauthor.co.uk

Starlight Children's Foundation

Starlight is a small children's Charity which has a massive impact on the lives of seriously ill children and their families throughout the UK. They are the only children's charity delivering services into every children's ward in hospitals and hospices throughout England, Scotland, Wales, Northern Ireland, the Channel Islands and the Isle of Man.

Starlight is there for those families in their time of need, lifting children's spirits in hospital, making dreams come true, strengthening family bonds and creating happy memories for everyone to share and cherish, whatever the future holds. We know that happy children respond better to treatment and each year we help over half a million children to forget about being sick or stuck in hospital and simply have some fun.

Thank you for your support

STARLIGHT
Brightening the lives of seriously and terminally ill children

Acknowledgements

I would like to say a huge thank you to everyone who has supported me with the books especially my family and friends.

Also to Helene Warren, Emma Kerridge, Holly Weaver and Barbara Boyd who helped me so much with the first edition of Harriet the Hedgehog and Harrison the Hedgehog. Without their help and hard work I would never have got them published.

I would also like to thank the talented Kim Whittingham whose illustrations, enthusiasm and support has been second to none.

Finally, I would like to say how proud I am of my beautiful nieces Megan and Gracie, who are now enjoying life to the full.

First published in 2013 by Victoria Brock
Second edition published in 2014 by Victoria Brock

ISBN 978-0-9927343-1-2